Dear Parent:
Your child's love of reading starts here!

Every child learns to read in a different way and at his or her own speed. Some go back and forth between reading levels and read favorite books again and again. Others read through each level in order. You can help your young reader improve and become more confident by encouraging his or her own interests and abilities. From books your child reads with you to the first books he or she reads alone, there are I Can Read Books for every stage of reading:

SHARED READING
Basic language, word repetition, and whimsical illustrations, ideal for sharing with your emergent reader

BEGINNING READING
Short sentences, familiar words, and simple concepts for children eager to read on their own

READING WITH HELP
Engaging stories, longer sentences, and language play for developing readers

READING ALONE
Complex plots, challenging vocabulary, and high-interest topics for the independent reader

ADVANCED READING
Short paragraphs, chapters, and exciting themes for the perfect bridge to chapter books

I Can Read Books have introduced children to the joy of reading since 1957. Featuring award-winning authors and illustrators and a fabulous cast of beloved characters, I Can Read Books set the standard for beginning readers.

A lifetime of discovery begins with the magical words "I Can Read!"

Visit www.icanread.com for information
on enriching your child's reading experience.

Transformers: Meet the Decepticons

TRANSFORMERS, the logo and all related characters are trademarks of Hasbro and are used with permission.

© 2007 Hasbro. All Rights Reserved.

Printed in the United States of America.

No part of this book may be used or reproduced in any manner whatsoever without written permission except in the case of brief quotations embodied in critical articles and reviews. For information address HarperCollins Children's Books, a division of HarperCollins Publishers, 1350 Avenue of the Americas, New York, NY 10019.

www.icanread.com

Library of Congress catalog card number: 2006935090

ISBN-13: 978-0-06-088828-2 — ISBN-10: 0-06-088828-8

❖

I Can Read!

READING WITH HELP 2

TRANSFORMERS™
MEET THE DECEPTICONS

Adapted by Jennifer Frantz
Illustrations by Guido Guidi
Based on the Screenplay by Roberto Orci & Alex
Kurtzman from a Story by Roberto Orci & Alex Kurtzman
and John Rogers

HarperCollins*Publishers*

Evil alien robots called Decepticons
have landed on Earth.

They are from the planet Cybertron.

The Decepticons fight
to take over the universe.
They won't stop until they win.
And their next battle
will take place here on Earth.

The Decepticons are Transformers.

They are robots that hide among us.

They pretend to be regular machines.

They are very tricky and very bad.

A friendly chopper
comes in for a landing.

But that chopper isn't what it seems.

It turns into a Decepticon named Blackout!

Blackout crushes steel cars.

His blasts wipe out anything in his way.

Blackout is full of nasty surprises.

He carries a robot named Skorponok.

Skorponok digs through the desert sand.

He can sense anything that moves.

He hunts like a scorpion.

He is dangerous.

Frenzy is a Decepticon, too.

He is very tricky.

He can turn into a radio or a boom box.

When he is a robot,

he can shoot metal discs.

Frenzy wants to make big trouble.

He shuts down all the computers

with his terrible scream.

Barricade is another bad guy.

He can transform into a police car.

Frenzy wants to come along.

He turns into the car's CD player.

They drive the streets
looking for trouble.

Megatron is the most powerful

of all Decepticons.

He is a metal giant.

He feeds on energy.

Megatron won't rest

until he finds the Allspark.

It is the Transformers' life force.

Megatron wants it all for himself!

Megatron transforms into
a supersonic jet.

He blasts off on his evil mission.

Megatron finds what he is looking for.

It's the Allspark!

He sends a signal

to the other Decepticons.

Decepticons come
from all over
to help their leader.
The Decepticon named Starscream
jets through the sky.

Bonecrusher and Brawl

rumble over the ground.

The Decepticons unite.

Blackout

Skorponok

Barricade

Frenzy

Together they are a deadly force.

Starscream

Bonecrusher

Megatron

Brawl

Who can stop Megatron
and his Decepticon army?
The Autobots!

Autobots are good Transformers.

Their leader is Optimus Prime.

They want to save Earth

from the evil Decepticons.

The battle for the Allspark
and for planet Earth is on.
The metal giants lock in battle.

Megatron takes a hit!

The Decepticons lose this battle!

They flee the planet.

For now the Earth is safe.